A HORSE
Named BANDIT

by Marilyn D. Anderson
illustrated by Estella Lee Hickman

Published by Willowisp Press, Inc.
401 E. Wilson Bridge Road, Worthington, Ohio 43085

Copyright ©1985 by Willowisp Press, Inc.

Printed in the United States of America

10 9 8 7 6 5 4 3 2 1

ISBN 0-87406-056-7

One

WHEN Donna Ferguson first joined our
class, I just knew I wasn't going to like
her. I mean, what kind of girl would wear cowboy
boots to school? She was obviously a horse nut,
and that was my department.

I was known as the most horse-crazy girl in the
fourth grade. It probably doesn't sound like much
to you, but at least I got noticed. Whether we
were drawing pictures or writing stories, everyone
knew what to expect of me. My real name is
Wendy, but the kids usually called me "Whinny,"
complete with sound effects. I secretly liked my
nickname.

My parents hoped I'd outgrow horses. They
kept paying for lessons, waiting for me to get

really good at something. Piano, gymnastics, baton twirling—they weren't fussy. But, no matter what I tried, I was cursed with being an average person. Maybe that's why I love horses so much. Horses don't care if you're good at anything or not.

As I was saying, my title of "number one horse freak" was pretty secure until Donna came along. Her bright orange T-shirt, told me I had a serious rival. The front of the shirt had a picture of running horses and the words, "I'd rather be riding." The back said, "I love horses," only there was a heart where the word love should have been.

Todd Phillips took one look at her and hissed, "Hey, Whinny, she's your kind." I pretended not to hear.

Our teacher announced that the girl's name was Donna Ferguson. Then the teacher appointed me to "make her feel at home." Thanks a bunch, I thought. The next recess I showed her where the bathroom was and stuff like that. I couldn't think of anything else to say. We were heading back to our seats when her eyes fell on a book lying on my desk.

"Oh, are you reading *A Horse at Last?*" she cried. "Isn't that good?"

"I'll say," I agreed. "I'd give anything to have a horse like Magic Moment."

From then on Donna and I found plenty to talk about. When we weren't comparing horse books, we were arguing about which breed of horse was the best. I went over to her house and she came to mine. We traded horse posters and spent hours plotting how we could get a real one.

That summer we tried hard to earn enough money to buy a horse. We sold garden seeds, peddled cookies, mowed lawns, washed cars, ran errands, and babysat. But we never came close to our goal.

By August our parents were so sick of hearing about the horse fund that they sent us to camp. The camp had horses! For Donna and me, camp was two weeks of heaven. They even had a horse show on the last day, and I won a ribbon. My folks were impressed.

School started soon after that. The horse fund was forgotten, but Donna and I did everything together. Then it was spring again, and my birthday was coming up.

Early one Saturday morning Mom burst into my room. "Wendy, get up," she urged. "Your father and I have a big surprise for you."

Suddenly I was wide awake and sitting up. "A surprise?" I echoed. "Is it my birthday present?"

"Yes," she said, nodding. "We're going to pick it up this morning, so hurry and get ready." I never moved so fast in my life.

"What is it?" I asked as I threw my clothes on.

But Mom just grinned and shook her head. "You'll see," she said as she slipped through the door.

I expected Dad to drive us to one of the shopping centers, but instead, he drove out of town. The farther we went, the more curious I got. Finally, we turned in at the gate of a run-down-looking farm. Goats, pigs, ducks, and cows ambled among the sagging buildings.

"What are we doing here?" I wondered, wrinkling my nose.

Dad looked at me sideways. "We thought you'd like a tractor for your birthday," he teased.

"Mike," my mother protested. "Don't be silly. This place may not look like much, but its horses have a fine reputation."

Then it hit me. "A horse?" I shrieked. "For me? Where is he?"

My parents both giggled then. "He's in the barn," said Mom, jumping out to lead the way to the largest building. The outside of the barn was badly in need of paint. But inside there was a row of clean, sturdy stalls. My mother headed for the third one on the left, and opened the door. The most beautiful brown and white horse I'd ever seen was looking out at us.

"His name is Bandit," she said. "He's a registered Appaloosa, and all his relatives are champions."

The horse studied me with large, intelligent eyes. He took a few steps forward to sniff my hands, and I patted his silky nose. His eyelashes were gorgeous.

"Is he really mine?" I asked. It seemed too good to be true. A horse of my own, and not just any horse, an Appaloosa, I thought. I'd read about the Nez Percé Indians and their famous spotted horses. The Appaloosa was said to be especially tough and good-natured. I even knew that Bandit's case-of-measles color scheme was considered valuable. As he nibbled my collar, I said, "I love him." And I meant it.

Mom looked very pleased. "Can you guess why they named him Bandit?" she asked.

I nodded. "That's easy," I said. "Those spots around his eyes look sort of like a mask."

My father arrived about then with an old man in faded denim work clothes. The man's weathered face and pointed hat made him look like a gnome from a fairy tale.

"Mr. Holcomb, this is my daughter, Wendy,"

9

Dad said, nodding in my direction.

The man gave a funny little bow. "Glad to meet you, Miss Dawson," he said. "Bandit, this girl is your new owner. What do you think of her?" he asked, as he stepped in front of the horse.

Bandit waved his head up and down as if he approved. "You're a good boy, aren't you?" the man went on. Again the horse nodded. Then Mr. Holcomb gave him a piece of carrot that had been hidden.

Dad applauded. "That's quite a trick," he said. "I'll bet you hate to sell him."

The man sighed. "I do for a fact," he agreed. "But I'm getting too old to fuss with horses. Bandit is the last of them, and he deserves to be used. Your wife tells me that you plan to show him."

I looked at Mom in surprise. I hadn't expected that. She was all smiles.

"Yes," she said. "Wendy will study with the best riding instructor we can find. I'm sure that she and the horse will win lots of ribbons."

Mr. Holcomb slapped his leg happily. "I hope you do," he said. "Yes, ma'am, that would be just fine."

Soon a truck and trailer came to take my horse to his new home. As soon as we arrived home, I began to wonder where we would keep him.

"Well, let's put him in the barn," Mom said, laughing.

"What barn?" I asked.

"Wait 'til you see," Dad said. He was grinning as he led the horse around behind the house. "I've fixed him a box stall in the old tool shed."

I was amazed. How had Dad done so much without my noticing? I wondered. The field out back was newly fenced. The outside of the shed had several new boards, and the inside was perfect as a stable.

"Gee . . . thanks," I told him.

Bandit walked quietly into his new home and began sniffing everything. When he was satisfied, he started munching hay.

"We'll let him explore the pasture later," Mom

said. "Right now he needs to relax."

"And we need to eat," Dad reminded her. "How about lunch?"

I was too excited to think about food. "Can I call Donna?" I begged. "She'll want to see my horse right away."

"I guess so," Mom agreed. "But you girls are not to ride Bandit today. I want him to be completely used to this place before you start riding him."

Two

DONNA refused to believe me at first.

"Sure you have a horse," she scoffed. "I'll be right over in my new Jaguar convertible to see him."

"But I do, Donna. I really do have a horse," I insisted.

"Describe it," she challenged.

"He's a brown and white Appaloosa, and his name is Bandit," I responded.

She considered that a moment. "Well," she said, "I still don't believe you, but I'll be right over." And she hung up.

Minutes later her bike tore into our driveway, and I swallowed the sandwich I was eating. Then I raced out the door yelling, "He's out back.

Follow me." We nearly scared poor Bandit to death as we dived in on him.

Donna's eyes were as big as the startled horse's. "See, see," I said, bouncing around excitedly. "Isn't he super? Aren't I lucky?"

For a minute I thought she was going to cry. "Yeah, I see," she said softly. "He's gorgeous all right, and you're the luckiest kid I know. Why couldn't I have gotten something like this instead of another baby brother?"

I ruffled Bandit's mane to hide my embarrassment. "Oh, Donna, you know you don't mean that," I scolded. "I'm going to share Bandit with you, and the three of us are going to have a great summer, aren't we, boy?" Bandit eyed the carrot I was holding in my pocket. He nodded enthusiastically.

"Gosh," said Donna, obviously impressed. "Does he speak English, too?"

"Naw," I confessed as I produced the carrot. "It's just a trick he knows."

"You rat," she giggled, and she punched me in

the arm. "When can we go for a ride?"

I shrugged and said, "Not today. Mom wants him to get adjusted to things around here first."

"How long will that take?" she asked.

"A few days," I guessed. By now Bandit had lost interest in us so we watched him eat for a while. Then Mom and Dad came out.

"Well, girls," Dad said. "Let's see what Bandit thinks of the pasture."

Mom looked a little nervous as she said, "I hope he respects our fences."

My hand was already on the stall door when Dad gave me the nod. I drew the bolt back and stepped out of the way as the door swung past. Bandit came to the opening and tiptoed out. He sniffed and snorted at every step.

Once outside, his body quivered with excitement. We waited for him to start running, but he never did. Instead, the horse merely dropped his head and began to graze.

"I can't believe this," Donna complained. "I thought we'd see a real explosion."

"Me, too," I agreed.

But Mom assured us, "It's much better this way. You should be glad you have a sensible horse." She and Dad watched for a while. Finally they went back in the house.

Donna and I flopped down in the grass not far from my beautiful, spotted horse. "You don't suppose he's lazy, do you?" I asked, chewing on a stem of timothy.

Donna rolled over on her back and stretched. "No, he's just sensible," she answered. "You heard your mom."

But I couldn't stand it. I had to see if Bandit would at least trot. I got to my feet and ran toward him, waving my arms. "Giddy up," I yelled. "Run, move."

The horse gave me a puzzled look and continued his grazing a little farther away. "All he wants to do is eat," I complained. "That's a bad sign."

"Forget it," said Donna. "Did your folks get you a saddle and bridle, too?"

"Yeah," I told her. "Want to see?"

She did, so we went in the house to drag out my new equipment. Since everything was dry as cardboard, we decided to use the sample of leather conditioner we found in the box. The directions said to take the saddle and bridle apart first, that part wasn't hard. Unfortunately, there were no directions on how to get things back together again. Donna and I were puzzling over a kitchen full of oily straps when we suddenly heard whinnying.

"Hey, that sounds like your horse," cried Donna. And we ran to the window.

It was Bandit, all right, and he didn't look lazy now. He was flying around the pasture yelling bloody murder. As he bore down on the fence closest to the house, I held my breath. Would he go through it or over it? I wondered. But inches away the horse slid to a stop. He barreled back the way he'd come.

"Mom, Dad, Bandit's going crazy," I screamed. "Come quick." They met Donna and me at the

17

back door, and we all raced out to stop the frantic horse. But there was nothing we could do. None of us were reckless enough to try to grab Bandit's halter. He continued at a mad gallop until he was sweaty and breathing hard. Then he merely paced the fence line. A violent whinny escaped him every few minutes.

My mother let out a long breath and said, "I'm glad that's over. He had me worried."

Dad nodded wisely. "The horse respects our fences," he said. "And I predict he'll get over that pacing pretty soon."

But Dad was wrong. Bandit continued walking back and forth and whinnying for hours. He sounded so terribly sad that I wished there were something I could do to comfort him. Donna and I gave him carrots and apples and told him how much we loved him. But it didn't do any good. The horse would stop long enough to eat and nuzzle our hands. Then he was back to his pacing.

Donna said she had to be home before dark.

My mom finally made me come in, too. I wondered how I'd ever be able to sleep with Bandit's cries haunting me.

About 10 o'clock I had finally finished putting the saddle back together. Then the phone rang, and Dad answered it. "Yes," I heard him say. "We did just get a new horse, and he is sort of unhappy right now. . . . Oh, yes, I understand, Mr. Steele. I'm sure it is very annoying. . . . Yes, well, I'll see if we can get him in the shed."

Dad looked worried when he hung up. "That was Mr. Steele," he said. "You know, the district attorney who lives a few houses down. He said we'd better do something about Wendy's noisy horse right away, or he will. Come on."

This time Bandit was easy to catch. He seemed pleased by all the attention my family gave him as we put him in his stall. As soon as we started to leave, he started screaming again. We had to shut tight all the doors and windows to muffle his cries. I felt terrible about leaving him.

The next day I fed Bandit and went off to

church. He seemed quieter after dinner, so we decided to let him into the pasture again. This time he didn't eat at all. He just started pacing and screaming immediately. It took the whole family to maneuver him back in the barn.

"What do we do now?" Dad fumed.

"I'll call Mr. Holcomb," Mom decided. "Maybe he'll have a suggestion."

Three

MR. Holcomb had a suggestion all right. In fact, he claimed to have a sure cure for Bandit's problem. We were to come to his farm right away and pick it up. Dad didn't want to go, so Mom and I set off on our own.

As we left the driveway, I said, "What do you suppose Mr. Holcomb has in mind?"

Mom shook her head. "That's hard to say," she answered. "The old man is a little strange, but everyone agrees that he knows horses."

We found Mr. Holcomb asleep in a chair on his front porch. He awoke, and stretched and yawned. "I'll be right with you," he said. We waited while he pulled on his ankle-high work shoes and laced them. "It's a long reach down these days," he told us, retrieving his hat from under the chair. He stood stiffly and ambled off. "Got just the thing to calm down that horse," he promised. From inside a small farm building, he produced a burlap sack. Something was moving inside! "Her name is Gracie," said Mr. Holcomb.

Mom and I stepped away from the sack. "Who or what is Gracie?" Mom sputtered.

The man winked at me. "Gracie is a Muscovy duck," he said.

Mom rolled her eyes. "But what would we want with a duck?" she asked.

The expression on his face showed that Mr. Holcomb thought we were pretty dense. "Bandit is lonesome," he explained. "The horse needs company, right? Well, would you rather have a goat or a pig or a duck?"

Mom opened her mouth to say something and changed her mind. Mr. Holcomb tried again. "You see, Bandit was raised with a barnyard full of animals. He misses his family. You adopt his cousin Gracie and your problems will be over."

My mother thought about that for several minutes. At last she said, "How much is the adoption fee?"

The man gave us a gap-toothed smile. "Five dollars," he announced, "and I guarantee my duck."

"Okay," Mom said with a sigh. "I don't suppose we have any choice."

Mr. Holcomb accepted the money cheerfully. "I figured you'd see it my way," he said.

Gracie didn't make a sound as the sack was dumped into our trunk. I heard one hiss of protest when the lid was shut, but Mr. Holcomb assured us she'd be fine.

We hadn't driven far when Mom began to giggle.

"What's so funny?" I asked.

Laughing all the harder, she managed, "Boy, are we dumb. We never even looked in the sack."

"I hope Dad thinks it's funny," I said. She stopped laughing.

Mom and I were dying to see if a duck really

would help Bandit. So, as soon as we got home, we hurried around to open the trunk. The trip must have ruffled Gracie's feathers because the sack immediately began to leap around. Strange, threatening sounds came from it.

"You'd better get Dad," my mother decided. "I'll keep an eye on the sack."

Dad was sprawled in front of the TV when I came flying in. At first he was too deeply engrossed in a baseball game to even notice me. "Dad," I cried. "Mom wants you right away. She needs help."

"Huh?" he grunted. "Where is she?"

"Out by the car," I told him. "Come on."

"All right," he said. "Don't get excited. I'm coming."

I raced back to the car to find Mom holding the trunk down with difficulty. Dad arrived a few minutes later. "What have you got in there?" he demanded.

"Never mind," Mom said anxiously. "Just carry it to the shed, please."

He frowned and tugged at the sack. "Awwwwwk!" it said, bouncing several feet in the air.

Dad leaped back. "Holy cow, it's alive!" he gasped. "Does it bite?"

"I don't think so," she said. "It's just a duck."

"A duck?" my father exclaimed. "Why a duck?"

My mother ran a hand over her face. "It's a long story," she said in a warning tone. "Just get it out of the trunk, okay?"

Dad muttered under his breath and pounced on the sack. This time he managed to heave Gracie out of the trunk before she knew what hit her. We were halfway to the shed before the duck could launch a new attack.

As the bag began to swing wildly through the air, I tried to help my father. Unfortunately, I got in his way instead, and we both fell in a heap.

My mother began to giggle again as she watched my dad and me and the sack rolling around on the ground. But the look on Dad's face as he turned around made her stop. "This isn't funny, Jean," he warned.

"No, of course, not," she said seriously. Dad picked himself up, pounced on the sack again, and raced desperately to the door.

"We'll just put Gracie in with Bandit now and see what happens," Mom said.

"What do you expect to happen?" Dad wondered.

"We don't know," I said. "But Mr. Holcomb claimed the duck would make Bandit less homesick."

Dad shook his head. "Sounds crazy to me," he said, opening the shed door.

It took the three of us to wrestle the sack into Bandit's stall. When Bandit saw the sack move on its own, I thought he might go through the roof. He backed into the far corner of his stall, shaking fearfully as Dad undid the string. Then Gracie blasted her way out in a storm of feathers, and I covered my eyes. When I dared look again, I saw that the duck had landed right under Bandit's nose. He was sniffing her eagerly while

she muttered complaints.

My father's eyes widened. "You call that a duck?" he scoffed. "It looks more like a vulture."

He had a point. Gracie was definitely the ugliest duck I'd ever seen. For one thing, she was enormous and very scraggly-looking. Worse yet, she had a fiery red patch of skin around both eyes that made her look down-right gruesome.

29

I shrugged. "Well, whatever she is," I said, "Bandit seems to like her."

My mother nodded. "The man guaranteed his duck," she added. "Let's just leave them together for a while."

"You'd think I was Old MacDonald," my father said with a sigh. "First a horse, now a duck. We may live in the country, but this is a housing development, not a farm. Remember that."

"Oh, Mike," said Mom. "This is all going to work out just fine. You'll see."

Dad put his arm around Mom as we started into the house. "I hope so," he said. "I certainly hope so."

Four

WHEN we checked on Bandit and Gracie again, the horse seemed a lot more relaxed. Dad thought it might even be safe to put him in the pasture again. So I opened the shed door and held my breath. Gracie strutted right out to inspect the place. Bandit followed meekly. Then, like old friends, they trotted side-by-side. We heard no more whinnying that night.

At breakfast the next morning, Mom was feeling rather smug. "Well, Mike," she said to my father. "Do you still think buying that duck was crazy?"

"Ask me again in a week or so," he answered, kissing her good-bye as he left for work.

Mom and I washed the breakfast dishes. She

agreed I should try riding my new horse. She had taken a few days off from her job to help me with Bandit.

It took us a long time to get a saddle and bridle on the horse. Since I'd only done it a few times at camp, I was all thumbs. My mother was full of advice, but she really wasn't much help.

At last I finished the job and started to lead Bandit out the door. Before we'd gone two feet, Gracie gave an angry squawk. The horse refused to move until she'd fluttered up to roost on my brand new saddle.

"Get off," I shouted, knocking her to the ground. "Who do you think you are, anyway? You dumb duck."

Gracie seemed surprised at my reaction. She backed up a few steps, but she continued to flap her wings and give me dagger looks.

My mother helped me check the girth. She held Bandit's reins while I swung up. I settled myself into the saddle and found the stirrups. Being on my very own horse at last was a wonderful feeling. It was so wonderful that I sat absolutely still for a few minutes just thinking about it.

"Cluck to Bandit," my mother said worriedly.

"I know," I said, picking up the reins. Then I nudged Bandit into a walk, and Gracie followed. We practiced turning, stopping, and starting. The duck stayed right at our heels. At first I was afraid she would get stepped on, but Bandit was watching out for her.

Soon I felt confident enough to ride to the farthest corner of the pasture. When we came trotting back, Gracie was crouched down. She muttered to herself when we passed her without stopping. After that she stayed put, and I forgot about her.

Bandit's trot was so rough that I tried something I'd learned at camp. "Up, down, up, down," I said to myself as I stood on every other beat.

My mom frowned as she watched us. "Wendy," she called. "Why are you going up and down so much?"

"It's called posting," I yelled back. "It helps to take the bounce out of the trot."

"Oh," she answered, sounding impressed. "Then I guess it's all right for you to do it, but I'll be glad when we get you a riding instructor."

After lunch I called Donna and invited her to come over about two o'clock. I wanted to impress her, so I got on Bandit before she arrived. Donna, however, barely noticed me at first. She was too busy looking at our duck.

"Where did that come from?" she asked.

"That's just Gracie," I said. "She's Bandit's babysitter."

"I see," Donna said skeptically. "And why does your horse need a babysitter?"

"He's a very young horse," I said, closing the subject. "Now tell me, what do you think of Bandit under saddle?"

"I think he's gorgeous, marvelous, and fantastic," she gushed. "So when do I get to ride him?"

I grinned and said, "Right now. I just wanted to

be sure you know how lucky you are."

My feet had barely touched the ground before Donna was in the saddle. Her face glowed as she rode Bandit all over the pasture. She showed no sign of wanting to give him back.

I was just about to accuse her of horse stealing when Bandit stopped and came to attention. His ears were pricked toward a row of houses beyond ours, and he stared intently.

Then I heard something, too. It sounded like screaming. "I'd better see what's going on," I called to Donna. "One of our neighbors might need help."

As I started across the field toward the sound, Donna followed on Bandit. "I'll go with you," she offered.

"No," I said. "You stay here with the horse." I slipped quickly under the fence and sprinted through Blanchards' backyard. I approached the fence around the Steeles' pool. The screams seemed to be coming from inside. What do I do now? I thought. I certainly didn't want to go

barging in on them without a good reason. On the other hand, someone could be drowning on the other side. I decided to find out.

Racing along the fence, I finally found a way in. I opened a little gate next to the house and poked my head through. The platinum-blonde Mrs. Steele was at the far end of the pool. She was wearing a bright pink bathing suit, and high heels. Her hands were over her mouth. She had stopped screaming for the moment.

The reason for her distress was quite obvious. It was splashing around and having a great time in the water. It was Gracie, our crazy duck. She'd taken over the pool.

No wonder Mrs. Steele was afraid. She'd probably never seen a big white bird with blood-red eye patches carry on like a dive bomber. Gracie would swoop down at the water, barely touch her feet in it, and wheel back to the deck to start over again. Water and feathers were everywhere.

I was tempted to just slip back out the gate

and pretend I'd never seen a thing. Heaven knows, I didn't want to claim that stupid duck now. I did feel sorry for Mrs. Steele. She didn't know that Gracie was basically harmless. Finally, I called to the woman. "Mrs. Steele, I'm over here. Is there something I can do to help?"

She pulled her hands from her face at once. "Yes," she screeched. "Call the police."

I knew we didn't want the police. "Um, hold on, ma'am," I told her. "I don't think that will be necessary." Frantically I looked around for an idea. I needed something long enough to reach Gracie if I was going to drive her away. A beach towel lay across Mrs. Steele's lounge chair, and I grabbed it. Then, cracking the towel, I charged down the side of the pool toward the duck.

Gracie stopped splashing and sized-up the situation. Mrs. Steele could see that there was hope. She grabbed a long pole lying by the pool. She waved it at Gracie, and together we drove the duck toward the gate.

Once Gracie was safely on her way, the woman

grabbed my hand and pumped it. "Oh, thank you," she gasped. "I don't know what I would have done if you hadn't come along."

"No trouble at all," I said grandly. "It's a good thing she doesn't know who owns that duck," I said to myself.

"How do you suppose that animal got in here?" Mrs. Steele wondered. "You don't think it will come back do you?"

I shook my head. "No, I don't think so," I said. "It probably just wandered in from a neighboring farm."

"Well," she continued. "I can't thank you enough, Miss . . . What did you say your name was?"

"Ah . . . Smith," I said quickly. "Sally Smith. I've got to be going now. Bye."

Five

WE couldn't afford to have Gracie return to the scene of the crime, so I knew I'd have to tell my parents about her right away. I wasn't too worried about what Mom would say, but Dad was going to be furious. He was already in the kitchen when I came in.

Mom looked up from setting the table. "How was your ride?" she asked.

"Ah . . . fine," I said, grinning desperately. Then I disappeared into the bathroom. I'll tell them at supper, I promised myself.

Dad, however, happened to look out the window as we were sitting down at the table. "Where's Bandit?" he asked, turning to me.

My mother had to have a look, too. "You mean,

he's not in the pasture?" she asked. "Wendy, did you put him in the shed again?"

"Yes," I admitted. "I thought I ought to lock him up with Gracie. You see, Gracie visited Mrs. Steele today."

Dad's mouth dropped open. "Mrs. Steele?" he sputtered. "How did that happen?"

I shrugged and made a face. "I don't know," I said. "I guess she just felt like taking a swim."

"In the Steeles' pool?" he almost whispered. I nodded. "Good heavens," he exploded. "Are they going to sue?"

"I don't think so," I answered as I played nervously with my fork. "I chased Gracie off without telling Mrs. Steele who I was."

Mom rolled her eyes. "Did she cause a lot of trouble?" she asked.

"Yeah," I admitted. "When I got there Mrs. Steele was cowering in a corner while Gracie was having fun."

My father grunted and shook his head. "I was afraid something like this would happen," he fumed. "We're getting rid of that duck tomorrow morning."

"Take it easy," my mother said. She put her hand on Dad's shoulder. "This is Gracie's first offense. Surely you can give her a second chance."

"Yeah, Dad," I said quickly. "She'd stay out of trouble if you built her a pen."

His fingers drummed an angry rhythm on the table as we waited for his answer. "All right," he said at last. "I'll build a pen for that disgusting bird, but she better not get into trouble again."

My father started work on the pen right after supper. The following morning he stayed home from work to finish the job. I brought him tools and handed him nails. My mother brought him coffee and tried to keep his spirits up. Finally the pen was ready, complete with an old dog house my mom had rounded up. It was time to get Gracie.

We found our duck perched on Bandit's back. Bandit was lying down, and they both seemed to

be asleep. Dad pounced on Gracie at once, but he hadn't counted on getting the horse excited. In the confusion, Bandit's front end came up which dumped my father on the floor. He found himself holding the duck and staring up at a rather frightening set of horse's teeth. Mom and I tried hard not to laugh as we pulled Bandit away.

Dad lost no time in dumping the duck in her new pen. He slammed the door behind her. "Take that, you miserable beast," he told her. Bandit was screaming his distress from the barn, and my father yelled at him to be quiet. Gracie shook out her feathers and looked about with an evil eye. Suddenly she flew at the fence and beat it with her wings.

"I'll bet she's never been in a cage before," said Mom.

"That's just too bad, isn't it?" my father said with a satisfied look on his face.

When her first attack failed, Gracie backed off to plot her next move. It came soon enough. This time she attacked the chicken wire with her bill.

Again she failed. Shaking her head angrily she flew to the roof of the old dog house to pout. That really made her look like a vulture.

"I think she's going to stay put now," Dad gloated. "You can let the horse out."

Thinking that poor Bandit had suffered enough I sprang to free him. The horse rushed out nickering encouragement to Gracie. Then he circled her pen looking for a way in. Its newness seemed to confuse him at first, but soon he began to lean against the wire. Next he started to gnaw at the wooden supports that held the pen together.

Dad waved his hands at Bandit yelling, "Get away from there. Leave that alone." But the horse merely moved out of reach and continued pestering the fence. Even when Mom and I went to help my father, we were no match for the determined Appaloosa.

My father pounded his fist against the fence in frustration. "Get the tools back out, Wendy," he ordered. "I'll have to put another 2 X 4 around

the whole thing before that horse tears everything down."

It was after two o'clock before Dad was ready
to leave for work. As he started out of the house,
he asked, "Wendy, do you really think this horse
is worth all the trouble?"

"Oh, yes," I assured him. "I love having Bandit,
and thank you very much for building the duck
pen. I'm going to spend the whole afternoon
riding."

"Good," said my father. "Then maybe Bandit
will be too tired to give me any more work to do."

Mom looked at the calendar and sighed. "Just
think," she said. "I have to go back to work
tomorrow. Wendy, can you handle Bandit well
enough now to be left alone?"

"Oh, sure," I told her. "He's a real pussy cat.
He won't give me any trouble."

She looked doubtful. "Then you won't mind if I
watch you ride today?"

"Watch away," I said confidently.

That afternoon Bandit was anything but a

pussy cat. He was so concerned about Gracie that he acted more like a mule. I could barely get him saddled because of his wiggling. He obviously didn't want me to ride. No amount of kicking would make him move away from the duck pen.

Mom frowned harder and harder as she watched. "You've got to show that horse who's boss," she told me. She brought me a green switch she'd broken off a nearby tree. "Use this on him."

I hated the thought of hitting Bandit even if he did deserve it, but luckily I didn't have to. One look at the switch was enough to get his attention off Gracie, and after that I could control him.

As Mom got ready for work the next day, I could see she was worried. "You've got to be extra-careful when you ride alone," she told me for the fifth time.

"I'm not riding alone," I said. "Donna is coming over."

My mother groaned. "That's even worse," she said. "You two are experts at getting into messes.

I'm glad I asked Mrs. Clark from next door to keep an eye on you."

"Aw, Mom," I objected. "Mrs. Clark is so old she'll probably expect us to be riding sidesaddle."

My mother checked her makeup in the hall mirror and said, "Wendy, you're exaggerating again. Now don't do anything to upset Mrs. Clark. I'll see you tonight."

"Okay," I said, returning her good-bye kiss.

Donna and I had a great time with Bandit that afternoon. We eventually got so brave that we were galloping him, but that brought Mrs. Clark on the run. She bobbed toward us in her lavender jogging suit, waving frantically for us to stop. I rode over to see what she wanted, and I got an earful.

"Wendy, I'm very upset with you," she scolded. "Your mother said I should keep track of you, and that makes me responsible for your safety. I saw you girls racing around the pasture. And I know you're taking unnecessary chances."

"We weren't racing," I explained. "We were just letting Bandit gallop. They let us do it at camp."

"I don't care," Mrs. Clark sputtered. "It looks dangerous to me. If you're not more careful, I'm going to have to call your mother."

I knew she would, too. So I said, "Okay, Mrs. Clark, whatever you say. Bandit is getting kind of tired anyway. What if we just stop riding for a while?"

She looked very relieved. "Yes," she agreed. "Yes, do something else. Watch TV or play a nice game."

So Donna and I unsaddled Bandit and rubbed him down. After we turned him loose, we had lunch. There wasn't anything good on TV, and we never were much for games. We kept busy with a deck of cards, but finally we got bored with it. Suddenly I had a terrific idea.

"You know what I'd like to do?" I asked dreamily.

Donna looked up. "No, what?"

"Take Bandit trail riding," I announced.

"Where?"

"In the woods behind the pasture," I told her. "Remember all those old trails we found last summer?"

Donna sat up to give the matter serious consideration. "Yeah," she agreed. "Those trails would be perfect for a horse."

We looked at each other silently as the clock ticked away the minutes. "It sure would be fun," I said.

"I remember seeing a gate on that side of the pasture, too," she added.

"You're right," I realized. "We could take Bandit right out that gate and have a blast." By now I was on my feet.

Donna got to her feet more slowly. "Aren't you forgetting something?" she asked.

"Like what?" I asked.

"Like Mrs. Clark," she said, giving emphasis to every word.

I frowned and thought hard. Then I had it.

"She'll never see us," I decided.

"Oh, yeah?" Donna challenged. "How come?"

I grinned at her. "Because Mrs. Clark will be too busy watching TV. She does exercises with Betty Bliss. If we get back before two-thirty, she'll never miss us."

At that point Donna raced me to the door. "So what are we waiting for?" she cried.

Six

GIGGLING like fools, Donna and I got Bandit ready. The temperature was already in the high 80s. We could hardly wait to get in the cool woods. Only a rusty gate stood in our way.

Donna held Bandit while I tackled the ancient wires. I tugged and tugged at the loop holding the fence, but the thing seemed to have grown into the fence post. I could not pry it off. When I gave up, Donna tried. She didn't bother trying to raise the loop. She just yanked at the gate until the rusty metal broke.

"Oh, oh," I said. "We'll have to fix that when we get back."

"Sure, sure, we'll fix it later," she agreed. "Come on." Donna led the way over the bushy

53

little ridge where the gate had stood. Bandit and I scrambled after her, but he kept looking back, snorting nervously. He'd have called to Gracie if I hadn't clapped my hand over his nose just in time.

"Let's get out of here," I urged. "We don't want Mrs. Clark to hear Bandit screaming. That would make her look out the window for sure."

Donna nodded. "Let me ride first, okay?"

I looked nervously at the trail ahead. "This part of the way is pretty rugged," I pointed out. "Maybe we should just lead him for a while."

"Don't be silly," she scoffed. Donna pulled herself into the saddle and kicked Bandit into action. I had to move fast to keep up. The trail went up and down and over fallen logs, under low branches and around piles of brush. Bandit and Donna easily made their way through it all until we came to a stream. There the horse stopped and whirled, determined to go back.

I caught Bandit's bridle and led him over to look at the water. Donna urged him forward with her heels. The horse refused to get his feet wet. Finally I broke off a switch and said, "Let me ride him."

When I mounted the horse, the sight of the switch in my hand was enough to make Bandit reconsider the stream and walk through it. When he stepped gingerly into the current, I let him have enough rein so that he could drink. He splashed the water with his nose and pawed at it with his front feet.

"He reminds me of my little brother at bath time," said Donna, standing up on the stream's bank.

"This is fun," I started to say. But suddenly I felt the reins pull. The horse's body begin to collapse.

Donna screamed, "Look out!" It was too late. The front end of the horse disappeared into the water, and I was soaked.

Luckily, I had my switch with me or he probably would have lain down completely. When I hit him with the switch, he bounded to his feet and plunged up the opposite bank. There he stopped to snort, and I surveyed my drenched clothes.

Donna started to laugh. I was about to say something nasty to her when Bandit began to shake himself like a big dog. What a feeling! My limp body was flung from side to side like a dish rag. If I hadn't held on to the saddle horn, I'd have fallen off for sure.

Donna fell on the ground laughing at our performance. "Some cowgirl you are," she howled. "It's a good thing you know how to swim."

I slid off Bandit and handed her the reins. "Very funny," I sniffed. "You ride him if you're so smart." My boots had water in them and my clothes stuck to me.

At last Donna stopped laughing. "I'm sorry," she said, "but if you could have seen the look on your face . . . "

"Never mind," I growled.

"Are you sure you want me to ride?" she asked

doubtfully, eyeing Wendy.

I nodded. "The saddle is so wet now you're welcome to it."

So she rode and I walked. After a while our narrow, overgrown trail met a wide well-traveled bike path. Donna stopped there and waited for me. "We could ride double here," she suggested. "This is a regular freeway after what we've been through."

I pulled some burrs off my socks and considered her idea. "How do I get on?" I wondered.

"Easy," she retorted. "I'll slide behind the saddle so you can use the stirrups."

I felt my squishy pants and eyed the wet saddle. "No, I have a better idea," I said. "You get off, and I'll get on. Then I'll get behind the saddle for you."

"Okay," she agreed, getting down. There was a wild confusion of arms and legs as Donna and I struggled to get on that saddle. We never would have made it if Bandit hadn't been so patient.

Then we were off again, free and looking for adventure. My pants finally dried and I was really beginning to enjoy myself. When I started to sing an old cowboy song, Donna joined in. As we passed under some low branches, I shredded leaves to throw in her hair. "Happy New Year!" I cried. She gave me an elbow in the stomach which made us both laugh.

I was so relaxed I wasn't even hanging on. Then I felt Bandit grow tense. He came to a quick stop and stared ahead fearfully. That's when I heard the sound of a motor. A three-wheeler, carrying two boys, zoomed into view.

Bandit panicked. He did a fast 180 degree turn and bolted back the way we'd come. "Stop him," I screamed at Donna, grabbing her desperately around the waist. But there was nothing she could do. The horse was out of control and picking up speed by the minute.

Glancing over my shoulder I was relieved to see that the boys had stopped. They were pointing at us and yelling. Then I was too busy

dodging branches to look anymore.

Soon we came to the place where our little trail left the big one. That's when things really got exciting. Now we were making hairpin turns around trees. We flew over huge logs. Donna and I were bouncing several inches off of Bandit's back. I landed as best I could and hung on.

Then we were tearing through the fence and across the pasture behind my house. I couldn't believe we were still on. Straight to the duck pen we galloped. I knew that Bandit would slow down soon, and he certainly did.

The horse threw on his brakes so fast that he bounced about four times. When he was quiet at last, I was hanging down his left side with my right foot waving in the air. Donna tried hard to keep us both up, but she couldn't do it. We plopped onto the ground with our bodies all tangled together.

I sat up and rubbed my hip. I probably would have cried if Donna hadn't been grinning like a jack-o'-lantern.

"Now that's what I call exciting," she cried. "That horse can really jump."

"So I noticed," I said with a groan. "Next time you get to ride the rumble seat." Then something made me look at my watch. "Good grief," I realized. "It's after two-thirty. What if Mrs. Clark saw us?"

We quickly scrambled to our feet. Donna said, "She'd have a coronary if she did."

"Let's cool this horse off and get cleaned up," I said, starting toward the barn with Bandit. We never made it because Mrs. Clark suddenly appeared.

"You girls!" she blustered. Her chubby body shook as she said it. "You girls are impossible. Wendy, just wait until I tell your mother."

Seven

I was speechless. If Mrs. Clark told my parents she'd seen us fall off a runaway horse, they'd have a fit. Donna and I would never be allowed to ride by ourselves again. What kind of an excuse could I possibly give her? I wondered.

Finally, Mrs. Clark shook her head in a bossy way and said, "Honestly. I don't know why you girls want to gallop around this pasture all the time. Why, when I was a girl, horses weren't play things. They were used to travel from place to place, and that was it." Then she turned, shook her head again, and walked away.

Donna shot me a look of disbelief. "She thinks we were just fooling around in the pasture," she crowed softly.

I put my finger to my lips and turned my back on Mrs. Clark's retreating figure. "Shhhh," I said. "We don't want her to find out how fast Bandit can really get from place to place."

That started Donna giggling, and I couldn't help giggling, too. I guess we were kind of punchy after all the excitement.

When we finally managed to stop laughing, Donna asked, "Do you think your mother will ground us?"

I shrugged. "That's hard to say. But we'd better finish cooling this horse off before he gets sick."

* * * * *

The telephone rang the instant my mother got home that night. I didn't offer to answer it because I knew it had to be Mrs. Clark. It was her all right, and my mother didn't get to say anything other than "Hello" for quite a while. The more Mom listened, the more she frowned.

The more she frowned, the more worried I got.

At last she said, "Well, thank you for calling, Mrs. Clark. I do appreciate your concern for Wendy, but try not to worry so much. You see, my daughter is planning to show her horse so she can't go slowly all the time. Yes . . . well, I'll talk to her. Good-bye, Mrs. Clark."

"Whew," I said to myself. We're off the hook. I knew my mother would want to give me a lecture, and I decided to make it easy for her. Since there was no doubt in my mind that I deserved one, I just hung around and waited. It turned out that she had plenty of things to say to me.

"Wendy, that was Mrs. Clark," she began. I nodded. "She says that she saw you and Donna riding double today and that you were going awfully fast." I nodded again. "Dear, I wish you wouldn't ride double. The person who's sitting behind the saddle has very little to hang on to and could easily fall off."

"Yes, Mom, I see what you mean," I said earnestly. "We won't ride double anymore."

She smiled and said, "That's good. Now I know you're bored waiting for your lessons to start, but it won't be much longer. Your father went to look at a used trailer today. If he buys it, we'll have a way to get Bandit to the riding instructor."

"Terrific," I said, and went to set the table. Now I really felt lucky. It seemed Mrs. Clark had seen our runaway after all, but the barn must have kept her from seeing us fall off.

For the next couple of days Donna and I were very careful when we rode. Things were pretty quiet around my house until Saturday morning. That's when Bandit disappeared.

He was always waiting near the duck pen when I came out with his breakfast, but not that morning. I put his feed in his box and called, but he didn't come. Gracie was too upset to notice the grain I gave her. I made a quick search of the pasture and noticed the open gate. Horrified, I realized that Donna and I had forgotten to fix it. Bandit may have been gone all night, I thought. Why, he could be any where by now.

I tore back to the house crying, "Mom, Dad, come quick! Bandit's gone!"

My parents put down the newspaper. They lowered their coffee cups in unison. "Are you sure?" asked my father.

"Did you check the whole pasture?" Mom wondered.

"Yes, I looked everywhere," I sniffed. "Please help me find him."

My mother got to her feet. "I'll be right with you," she promised. "Just let me put on some old shoes."

"I hope he isn't bothering the neighbors," Dad said worriedly. He put his coffee cup in the sink and started for the door. "Do you have any idea how he got out, Wendy?"

I knew I had to tell the truth. "Yes, I think so," I admitted. "The old gate to the woods fell down a few days ago. I forgot to mention it."

My father turned to me and scowled. "I don't believe this," he fumed. "The fence falls down, and no one tells me. I just don't believe it."

Mom was ready by then, too. The three of us started out across the pasture together. Minutes later we were staring at the place where the old gate had stood. "It's down all right," my father observed. "I guess those rusty old hinges just gave out. The horse must be somewhere in the woods."

"But how will we ever find him?" I wondered.

Dad shrugged, and he surveyed the ground worriedly. "That might be difficult," he agreed. He had gone only a few feet more when he pointed and said excitedly, "Look. It's a hoof print."

Mom quickly joined him on the ground. "It's a horse's print," she said confidently, "but not a very fresh one."

My father made a face at her. "How do you know?" he snorted.

She stuck her chin in the air and said, "You don't believe me? I'll have you know I was the best wildlife tracker in Brownie troop #178."

My father sighed and got to his feet. "Forgive me, Princess Know-It-All," he said with a little bow. "Do tell us more."

"Well," Mom said, studying the hoof print from every angle, "This track was made by a horse moving very fast. I'd say he was coming rather than going."

Gosh, I thought to myself. She really does know tracking. I'll bet that track is from when Bandit spooked at the three-wheeler.

Dad refused to believe her. "Now I know you're crazy," he half-laughed, dragging her to her feet. "There are no wild horses in this woods that I know of, and Bandit hasn't come home yet. Forget the tracking, and let's just look for him."

We walked for quite a while, but we found no more hoof prints. The farther we walked, the more worried I got. Finally I said, "We'll never find Bandit this way."

"You're right," Dad agreed, and we all came to a stop. "It would take us a month to cover these woods. We'd better go back in case someone is trying to call us about him."

"What do we do if no one calls?" Mom asked.

"I'm not sure," he said with a sigh.

My mind began to work feverishly. I had to think of a plan. After all, Bandit was my horse. Then suddenly I had it, a way to locate him. "Gracie would know where to look," I shrieked. "And he'd come to us for sure if she were along."

Mom's face lit up. It might work at that," she said, hugging me hard. "Only we've got to find some way to keep track of her while she's looking."

"How about a leash?" Dad snorted. "If she's going to impersonate a bloodhound, she ought to dress like one."

"Good idea," my mother decided. "There's an old dog leash in the garage."

When we got home, Dad went to the house to wait by the phone. Mom and I quickly found the leash and rigged it up to give us control over the duck. That wasn't the easiest job I've ever helped with, but at last we were ready.

"Here goes nothing," Mom said and opened the door of Gracie's pen.

With a flurry of beating wings, the duck rushed out. I barely managed to hang on to the leash. But then, Gracie just stopped. Her long neck twisted back as she scornfully studied the harness we'd rigged for her.

"Go, Gracie," I yelled. "Find Bandit."

She rolled a red-rimmed eye at me, plopped on her bottom, and sulked.

I tried again, more politely this time. "Please, Gracie," I begged. "Please show us where Bandit is."

At that the duck rocked back to her feet and waddled slowly toward the barn. I could tell by the way she moved that she didn't know where Bandit was either.

Eight

G RACIE, Mom and I circled the barn
completely, and things were still looking
hopeless. The duck seemed to be getting more
concerned, but was evidently as confused as we
were.

Mom shook her head worriedly. "Maybe if we
took Gracie out to the gate, she could go on from
there," she suggested.

So, with me dragging on the leash and Mom
shooing from behind, we managed to maneuver
the duck toward the woods. As we approached
the gate, Gracie suddenly came to life. She
leaped into the air so quickly she pulled the leash
from my hands. She passed the gate in short
bursts of flight and kept on going. We raced

after Gracie. The farthest corner of the pasture was just ahead.

Then I heard a horse nicker from somewhere very close. It was soft and sounded discouraged. Something moved in the bushes next to the fence. It was Bandit! His spotted hide was a perfect camouflage. I was so happy to see him that I started to cry.

Gracie reached him first. She hopped on his back and began to scold him like a worried mother. I ran to the horse's head saying, "Bandit, what's wrong? Why didn't you come home?"

He turned to sniff my hands, but he seemed rooted to the spot. Then I saw why. His hoof was caught in one of the lowest wires of the fence. Getting down for a closer look, I found he wasn't really hurt. The wire had gotten stuck between his hoof and his shoe.

My mother arrived then, panting hard. "Is he all right?" she demanded as she tried to see over my shoulder. "Do you see any blood?"

"He's okay so far," I assured her. "But we'll

have to cut him out of this fence."

"What a mess," she gasped. "I'd better get your father. Now you be careful. Don't try to get him loose yourself."

So she went for help while I stayed with Bandit. I knew that he could still hurt himself if he got excited. I stroked his neck soothingly and said encouraging things to him. Gracie's leash was getting in the way so I took it off.

After what seemed like a long time, my parents came. Mom helped me hold Bandit's halter while Dad set to work using a wire cutter. Good ol' Bandit never moved a muscle, and he was free in no time. A last snip of the fence convinced him that things were normal again, and he moved away. Gracie hopped off to follow him to the shed.

"Whew, I'm glad that's over," I said, letting my whole body hang loose.

"Me, too," Mom agreed. "It's a good thing we found him when we did."

"Gracie knew where to look," I reminded her.

"She makes a pretty good bloodhound, doesn't she, Dad?"

My father was busy repairing the fence, but he looked up and smiled. "Yeah, I guess she does," he admitted. "In fact, I think she finally did something right."

Donna and I couldn't ride Bandit again until a farrier had come to reset his loose shoe. After that we made up for lost time. Every day we rode him around the pasture for hours. That was fun, but we kept dreaming of another ride in the woods. Finally, I got up the nerve to ask Mom about it. She frowned. She worried about us getting hurt, just the way I expected her to.

"Aw, Mom," I begged, "there are lots of neat trails back there."

She looked skeptical. "And lots of brush and junk for a horse to get tangled in, too," she pointed out.

"It's not that bad," I said. "Bandit's sure-footed, and we'd be careful." At least she hasn't said "no" yet, I thought.

"There is a biker's path on the other side of the woods that you would have to stay off," she said.

"Sure, Mom," I promised.

"And you'd have to take turns walking because I don't want you riding double."

"Right," I agreed.

Finally she said "yes," and for the next few weeks things were perfect. Having a horse was as wonderful as I had always dreamed it would be. Donna and I tied food to the saddle and had picnics. Some days we took turns jumping him over logs. We looked for buried treasure and scouted for Indians. Soon we knew where every trail led.

Then came the day when Dad bought a horse trailer. My mother immediately signed me up for riding lessons, starting the following Saturday. She was pretty excited about the whole deal, too.

"Wait until you see Miss Wilson's trophies," she bragged. "The woman has three cases of them. People say you almost have to audition to get lessons from this instructor."

"Can Donna go along?" I asked.

My mom shook her head and said, "Not this time. I want you to really concentrate on these lessons, not fool around."

"I'll try," I promised. This was sounding too much like gymnastics class to suit me.

That week I was too busy to go riding in the woods. Donna came over every day, but all she got to do was play teacher. As I rode circles around her in the field, she would tell me what to do next. By Friday night Bandit was working so well I was sure Miss Wilson would be impressed.

But Saturday started out all wrong. It was drizzling when we tried to put Bandit in the trailer. He was in a cranky mood and refused to get in. Nothing helped until we put Gracie in a crate and set it in the front of the trailer. Then he slowly stepped in.

We were late getting away, and it was raining hard as we left the driveway. "It's a good thing Miss Wilson has an indoor arena," my mother said as she nervously steered the unfamiliar load.

I think we were both relieved when we came to a big red and white sign that said "Wilson's Quarter Horses." We drove down a tree-lined lane until we came to a huge red pole barn. Mom parked right next to it, and we dashed in. We found ourselves at one end of a long row of white box stalls. I saw that each stall door held a brass name plate, a red bucket, and a matching blanket.

"Gosh," I exclaimed. "A color coordinated barn."

"Wait until you see the office," Mom said as she herded me to a doorway hidden between two stalls. We stepped right from the barn into a carpeted room complete with plush furniture. The trophy cases my mother had mentioned lined one whole wall. At one end of the room was a desk, and behind it sat an elegant-looking woman. I doubted she'd ever heard of dirt or rain.

The woman looked up from her books and

smiled at us. "Oh, Mrs. Dawson," she said. "I was beginning to wonder if you would make it."

"Sorry we're late," Mom apologized, "but the horse wouldn't load. I'd like you to meet my daughter, Wendy. Wendy, this is Miss Wilson."

I dried my hands on my damp jeans as the woman came toward me, her palm out-stretched. "So happy to meet you, Wendy," she said, shaking my hand formally. I murmured something in return, and she went on. "Now, where did you park?"

"Next to the row of stalls," Mom told her.

"Oh, dear," said Miss Wilson. "You're going to be in the way of the feed truck there. Please pull around to the other side of the barn before you unload. You can saddle your horse at the cross-ties over there."

Mom and I nodded and charged back out into the rain. We moved the trailer, carried in my riding equipment, and then unloaded Bandit.

He backed out in a big hurry, all bug-eyed and snorty. I got splashed full of mud as he pranced around trying to see everything. Then he neighed frantically until we took Gracie out, too. As we ran through the rain I had to laugh at Mom. She was trying to keep Gracie dry.

Miss Wilson was watching all this from within the building. When Mom carried the crate right past her nose, she couldn't stand it any longer. "What is that?" asked Miss Wilson.

I was following along behind with Bandit. "A duck," I said.

"A duck?" she repeated.

Nine

IT was embarrassing to have to explain Gracie to Miss Wilson. "The duck helps Bandit stay calm," I mumbled. "She's sort of like a pacifier."

"Hmmm," she said, watching the horse fidget. "It does look as if he needs some moral support. All right, but do keep that crate away from the other horses."

The lesson went terribly. Miss Wilson yelled at us constantly. Bandit was excited and wanted to go much too fast. Miss Wilson said I held my left shoulder too high, my toes stuck out, I slouched in the saddle, and more. I was sure she hated me.

At last it was over, and I went to unsaddle Bandit. My poor mother went to Miss Wilson's office to hear the verdict on my riding. I felt bad about letting her down.

Mom gave a nervous little laugh when she asked, "Well, is there any hope for Wendy?"

Miss Wilson seemed surprised at the question. "Of course," she said. "You have a very nice Appaloosa there, and your daughter gets along well with him. They won't win ribbons without a lot of work, but . . . "

"Oh, Wendy is a good worker," Mom assured her. "Just tell me what you want her to do, and I'll see that she does it."

Miss Wilson nodded. "All right," she said. "Here's the way it has to be: Wendy must ride at least an hour every day. She should work circles at the trot and canter until the horse learns to slow down. Keep reminding her about her posture. Bandit must be kept inside during the day so that his coat gets in better condition. He should be brushed for twenty minutes daily. I'll sell you some vitamins that will help, too."

"Okay," Mom agreed. "We can do those things."

"And one more thing," Miss Wilson added.

"What's that?" my mother asked.

"No one is to get on this horse but Wendy," Miss Wilson said firmly. "We don't want him confused by other riders."

Mom quickly agreed to that condition, too. They came out to the barn and explained everything to me. Miss Wilson finished by saying that winners were just people who wanted to win more than anyone else. "You *do* want to win, don't you, Wendy?" she asked.

One look at my mother and I knew what I had to say. "Uh, sure. I want to be a winner," I told her.

"And do you promise to follow the rules I've laid out?" she continued.

I squirmed a little, but I ended up saying I would. Mom seemed really excited about the way things had gone. She talked all the way home about how proud she was of Bandit and me. I didn't say much, though. I was too worried about what to tell Donna. She liked to ride Bandit, too.

How could I tell her she couldn't ride him anymore? I wondered.

We'd been home about an hour when the phone rang. "Oh, you're home," said Donna's cheerful voice. "Well, what did you learn at your lesson?"

"Lots of things," I hedged.

"Like what?" she asked.

"That I should sit up straight and keep my toes in," I said.

"Is that all?" she asked doubtfully.

"Well, no," I admitted. "I'm supposed to teach Bandit to slow down. That's the main thing I have to work on this week."

"How come?" she wondered.

"Miss Wilson says that western pleasure is the opposite of a race," I remembered. "The slowest horse usually wins."

"Hmmm," said Donna. "That's kind of weird, but why don't I come over this afternoon and help you work on it?"

I hesitated. "I'd like that," I said. "But I've got

some bad news for you."

"Bad news?" she repeated.

"Yes," I said miserably. "Oh, Donna. Don't get mad at me because this wasn't my idea. Miss Wilson said no one was supposed to ride Bandit anymore but me."

She didn't answer right away, and I wasn't surprised. I knew how I'd feel. Finally she said, "Oh," very softly. "Then I guess I can't help you, can I?"

"I'm really sorry," I told her as I tied the phone cord in knots.

"It's okay," she answered coolly. "I know it's not your fault. Well, I have to go now. See you around."

"Yeah, see you around," I said as she hung up.

Even though Donna had a right to be upset, I figured we could still be friends. I figured wrong. She never called me after that, so I tried calling her. It was weird. Suddenly we had nothing to talk about. Still, I wanted to stay friends, so I begged until she agreed to come over. When she came, she didn't stay long. We brushed Bandit for a while and she watched me ride a bit. Then she said she had to babysit for her mother. I hated to see her go.

The summer was boring without Donna. She and my other friends were busy with swimming and ball games. All I had time for was Bandit. His stall always needed cleaning, and Mom encouraged me to ride twice a day if possible. Day after day I made circles with that horse until we were dizzy. It wasn't fun, but at least I seemed to be making progress. Miss Wilson didn't yell at me so much, and Mom told everyone how well I was doing. I seemed to be doing something right at last.

Then I noticed a change in Bandit's personality, a change for the worse. Every day he seemed to resent the circles more. When I tried to saddle him, he laid his ears back and threatened me with his teeth. He blew his belly so full of air that I couldn't get the girth tight. He chewed the wood in his stall until it looked as if a beaver lived there. When I rode him, he moaned and groaned. He seemed to be awfully tired. Our training sessions became one big argument. I didn't say anything to Mom about it because I knew she'd think I was just making excuses.

The summer went quickly, and school began. Suddenly I was swamped. Between morning chores, evening chores, cleaning the barn, going to school, and doing homework, I was going crazy. Bandit and I grew to really hate our practice sessions because I was tired and cranky.

Our lessons weren't going well either. Bandit acted so lazy that Miss Wilson gave me some spurs and ordered me to use them. The spurs did get results, but I could feel Bandit's growing resentment.

Then one morning I overslept. I got up so late that I threw my clothes on, gave the animals their feed, and ran to school. Breathless, I slid into my seat just as the bell rang. The teacher had started taking roll when I caught Todd Phillips looking at me strangely. I pretended not to notice, but he poked one of the other boys, and they both stared.

I shifted around in my seat and did some fast checking. Yup, my buttons all seemed to be buttoned. My zipper was up. I pretended to read a book, but I could see that now some girls were giggling at me.

Tapping the girl ahead of me on the shoulder, I whispered desperately, "Susie, turn around. Why is everyone laughing at me today?"

She glanced back over her shoulder and quickly faced front again. "Your hair seems to be growing hay," she hissed back. Then she started to giggle, too.

Trying to act nonchalant, I reached up to feel the top of my head. I felt something dry and brittle. A small storm of stems landed on my desk. I wanted to die.

About that time Todd held his nose and said, "What's the matter, Whinny? Did you have to sleep in the barn?"

Our teacher, Mr. Bennett, happened to see

that. "Settle down, back there," he ordered. Everyone's noses quickly disappeared into books.

Nothing more was said to me until recess, but then I heard plenty. One boy called me a hayseed, and Todd claimed I looked like a horse. Some girls pretended to pick things off of my clothes as a joke. It was awful, and I was in a really rotten mood by the time I got home. Maybe that's why Bandit and I had such a big battle that night.

Ten

I was in no mood for silliness as I went out to ride that evening. When Bandit didn't move off fast enough for me, I gouged him with my spurs. He began to prance and toss his head which gave me an excuse to hit him with the reins. He grunted angrily. Then he stopped dead and refused to move at all. I reacted by losing control completely. Attacking him with both reins and spurs, I screamed, "I hate you, you stupid horse."

I could feel an explosion building under me, and suddenly it came. Bandit gave a mighty bellow as his head went down and he started bucking. On his first jump, I was thrown badly off balance. On his second, I hit the ground with a

jolt that knocked the wind out of me. For a few terrifying seconds, I was looking up at hooves just missing my head. Then it was over. Everything was very still, and I knew I failed again.

I didn't even try to get up at first. Although my rump hurt badly, I was reasonably sure nothing was broken. I knew I should catch Bandit and get back on. Instead, all the unfairness of the day washed over me, and I started to cry. "I can't do this," I blubbered to no one in particular. "I won't do it. You can't make me." Oh, I had a first-class pity party for myself. I almost hoped Mrs. Clark would come out and feel sorry for me. Maybe she'd tell Mom what a terrible horse Bandit was, and he'd be sold. It would serve him right.

But Mrs. Clark never did notice me, and gradually I got tired of crying. Finally I sat up and began to wonder what had happened to my horse. He hadn't gone far. Standing there nose to beak with Gracie, he looked as miserable as I felt. That's when it started to dawn on me that he might be frustrated, too. After all, he had to put

95

up with me every day, and he didn't even know what we were trying to prove.

I wasn't interested in riding him anymore that day, but I figured maybe I owed Bandit an apology. Dragging myself to my feet, I went over to him and stroked his neck for the first time in weeks. "I'm sorry," I told him. "I really don't hate you, and I know it's not your fault we have to make all these dumb circles. Maybe neither one of us is cut out to be show performers."

That night I had trouble concentrating on my homework. I kept thinking about Bandit and feeling guilty. At least my math was easy, but then I had to write something for English. Mr. Bennett was always having us read what we'd written for the class, and I hated it. This time we were supposed to write TV commercials. He figured we were all experts.

I chewed my pencil and wracked my brain for an idea. Should I try to sell soap or toothpaste or breath freshener. . . . Then it came to me, an inspiration. My pencil flew over the paper.

The next day, when it was my turn, I read:

"Ladies and gentlemen, are you tired of walking to school? Do your parents fight about who has to take you? Well, here's a way to beat the morning traffic. Get a new three-speed Appaloosa with power steering. Buy yourself a horse, and get a kick out of life."

The class laughed and applauded as I sat back down. Mr. Bennett even seemed to like my speech. He kind of smiled and said, "That was very good, Wendy. Now tell us the truth. You don't really want to sell your horse, do you?"

I thought for about two seconds and decided. "Yes, I do," I said. "Riding just isn't fun anymore, and the work is too hard."

I must have sounded pretty upset because everyone got quiet after that. Mr. Bennett called on someone else to read, and the class went on. Before long it was time to go home. The kids in my class always stampede for the front door as soon as the bell rings. I usually do too, but this time I hung back. I felt I just had to be alone for a while. The bathroom seemed like a good place to hide out. As I headed for it, Donna caught up with me.

"Wendy, wait," she said, tugging at my arm. "I want to talk to you."

"Not now," I said, without slowing down.

"Yes, now," she insisted, and she followed me through the door. "I want to know what's going on with you and Bandit. Are you really going to sell him?"

Well, I finally broke down and told Donna the whole story. It was great to have someone to talk to again. Before I finished I was crying. She helped me wash my face, and we started home together.

As we walked along Donna kept shaking her head. "This is all so stupid. We were having such a good time with Bandit before the horse show nonsense came up," she said.

"I know," I said miserably. "And now Mom and Dad expect me to bring home ribbons. I'm going to let them down again, I know I am. Oh, what am I going to do, Donna?"

"Tell them you don't want to show," she suggested.

"I can't," I wailed. "They'd think I was copping out on them."

"Then you've got to let me help you," she decided. "I'd be willing to do some of the work if I got to ride Bandit in return."

"Gee, I'd like that," I said at once. "But I don't think my mom would go for the idea." Then I gave the matter more thought. I just had to have some help. It was great to know Donna still wanted to be friends. I wouldn't mind sharing Bandit again either, but Mom would kill me if she caught Donna riding my horse. There was also the matter of my promise to follow Miss Wilson's rules. But the fact was that things couldn't go on the way they had been. I was tired and frustrated. If Donna didn't help, I'd just have to sell Bandit. No matter what I'd said before, I didn't want that now.

"Okay," I said at last. "If one of us rides while the other cleans the shed, it might work. We could alternate nights and finish in plenty of time before Mom comes home from work."

"Sounds good to me," she agreed.

So it was settled. I was happy for the first time in weeks. I felt so good that I told Donna she could take her turn at riding first. Actually it wasn't such a great sacrifice on my part. After the battle I'd had with Bandit the night before, I wasn't too keen on riding him again right away. Donna took me right up on the offer and had the horse saddled in record time. She stopped for a pow wow with me before she rode off.

"Is it okay if I ride him in the woods?" she asked, eyeing my wheelbarrow full of dirty straw. "It sounds to me as if he's ring sour. I thought a change of scene might do him good."

I started to say my mother wouldn't like it, but changed my mind. What difference did it make? At least they would be out of sight among the trees. "Okay," I told her. "Only be careful."

Laughing, she answered, "Now you sound like your mother. Bye." As she walked Bandit toward the gate leading to the trails, I noticed a new spring to the horse's step.

I finished my work with plenty of time left for a little nap on the patio. The next thing I knew Gracie was announcing Bandit's arrival, and Donna was grinning at me from the other side of the fence. "He was super today," she said breathlessly. "He's just like he used to be."

About that time I started looking forward to my turn on the fiery little Appaloosa. My ride would be in the woods also, I decided. After all, people can get ring sour, too.

The next evening was even better than I had hoped. With Donna taking care of the dirty work, I could play at last, and Bandit was wonderful. He cantered, jumped logs, and splashed through the stream with such enthusiasm that I was glad to be alive. I had to force myself to go home.

For the next several weeks our plan worked perfectly. The shed was cleaner than ever before,

Bandit was his old cheerful self again, and I had my best friend back at last. I even had time to goof off sometimes on the way home from school. I felt like a normal kid again.

Then one night, when it was Donna's turn to ride, I stopped for ice cream with some other kids. I was running a little behind and I hurried up our driveway. Suddenly, I saw something that gave me a shock. Mom's car was in the driveway! She'd come home early!

Eleven

MY mother met me at the door with a wild look in her eyes. "What's going on here?" she demanded. "Wendy, where have you been? What's happened to Bandit?" Sounds came out of my mouth, but they didn't make any sense.

She went on. "I had a doctor's appointment today so I came home early. When I found that you and the horse were both missing, I was upset. I didn't approve, but I figured you'd taken him in the woods so I wasn't really worried." She stopped for a breath. "Now you show up without Bandit. He's not in the barn because I checked. I'm afraid he's been stolen."

I cleared my throat and started to say something, but she interrupted.

"Of course, we need to be sure of that before we call the police," she rattled on. "I think we should have Gracie play bloodhound again. Maybe we can dig up some clues."

"I ought to stop her," I told myself. "I'd better tell her what really happened." But my mother isn't easy to reason with when she's excited, and she was very excited. She was halfway out the door before I could think of what to say. All I could do was to follow her and hope for the best.

Minutes later we were hurrying across the pasture with Gracie straining at the leash. As we reached the gate to the woods, my mom stopped suddenly and pointed. "Look," she almost whispered. "That fence has been folded back. Bandit didn't do that by himself."

I started to say, "Well, I think I know . . . " But she shoved the leash in my hand and got down for a closer look. "There," she said triumphantly. "See that, a fresh hoof print and the tracks of a person with very small feet."

Just then Gracie began to kick up a fuss. I

looked up to see Donna and Bandit coming toward us at a gallop. Sliding the horse to a stop, Donna bubbled, "Wendy, you should have seen the log we jumped today!"

Suddenly Bandit's head shot up. He shied and snorted. My mother was no longer on her hands and knees. She was standing behind me, and she was angry.

"Donna," she cried. "What are you doing on that horse?"

Immediately Donna slid to the ground and waited for me to explain.

"Uh . . . she's been helping me with Bandit," I stammered.

My mother's eyes narrowed. "I can see that," she said crossly. "You know Miss Wilson's rules."

I nodded and looked at the ground as she continued. "Are your riding lessons going to be like all the other things you started and didn't finish? At least we didn't have to feed the piano when you got tired of that!"

I bit my lip to keep from crying. Yes, I'd let

Mom down again, I thought.

Then my mom sighed and lowered her voice. "I know you're getting tired of working so hard, Wendy. It hasn't been easy, but soon it will all be worth it. At your last lesson Miss Wilson told me she plans to enter you in a show very soon. Isn't that exciting?"

I shook my head miserably. "I don't want to go," I blurted out.

Mom's eyes opened wide. "Of course, you do," she insisted. "This is what you've been working for all summer."

"I don't want to go," I repeated.

"But why?"she demanded. "Your lessons have been going so well. I figured you would be all excited about winning some ribbons."

"I don't care about that," I told her, "and I never did. Every time I start to enjoy something you want me to enter a contest. Then it turns into work and it's no fun anymore."

My mom's mouth fell open. "But contests are fun," she protested.

"Not to me," I said stubbornly.

"What do you mean?" she wondered.

I squirmed and looked at the ground again. "Oh, I don't know," I said. "It's just that I always disappoint you and Dad."

"Don't be silly," my mother protested. "You just need a little more practice, that's all."

"No," I said, meeting her eyes for the first time. "I want you to be proud of me. I can't be the kind of daughter you want. I've tried, but it's no use."

That's when her attitude really changed. She sniffed a few times and began to stare at me as if I was someone she hardly knew.

"But, Wendy," she said softly. "Your father and I are very proud of you the way you are. Surely you must know that."

I didn't believe her. She must have realized it because suddenly she put her arms around me. "Oh, honey," she said, squeezing me hard. "If we've been that pushy, I'm sorry. You don't have to win contests to make us love you. You're our little girl, and we'll always be crazy about you no matter what you do."

This time I could tell that she meant what she was saying, and it made me feel good all over. "Does that mean I don't have to be in any horse shows?" I asked hopefully.

"Of course," she answered at once. "We only started this business with Miss Wilson because we thought it would make you happy."

Right then I could see things were going to turn out just perfect. "Then you wouldn't mind if I stopped taking lessons?" I insisted.

Mom laughed and shook her head. "Not at all," she said. "In fact, your father will be delighted. He's been complaining about the expense ever since we started."

I looked over at Donna, and we both just beamed with happiness. "Hurray!" I yelled. "Then Donna can ride Bandit whenever she wants, and no more circles."

"Trail riding, here we come," she cheered.

"And no more shed to clean," I realized.

"Bandit will be able to spend every day in the pasture now." Then turning to Bandit, I asked, "Isn't that great, fella?"

He nodded his head and whinnied so loudly that Gracie hissed at him.